# Howdy Doody IN FUNLAND

BY EDWARD KEAN

PICTURES BY ART SEIDEN

SIMON AND SCHUSTER • NEW YORK

THE LITTLE GOLDEN BOOKS ARE PRODUCED UNDER THE SUPERVISION OF
MARY REED, PH. D.
FORMERLY OF TEACHERS COLLEGE, COLUMBIA UNIVERSITY
THIS IS A BRAND-NEW BOOK, WRITTEN AND ILLUSTRATED ESPECIALLY FOR GOLDEN BOOKS

Once again Howdy Doody and his friends bring you lots of fun with a merry adventure, this time in Howdy's Doodyville Park. The pictures are by Art Seiden, whose most recent Little Golden Book is HOWDY DOODY AND THE PRINCESS.

 Designed and produced by The Sandpiper Press and Artists and Writers Guild, Inc. Printed in the U. S. A. by Western Printing and Lithographing Company.
Published by Simon and Schuster, Inc., Rockefeller Center, New York 20, N. Y.
Published simultaneously in Canada by the Musson Book Company, Ltd., Toronto

IT WAS Opening Day at the Doodyville Park, with Howdy Doody in charge. Howdy and Dilly Dally and Clarabell Clown had really been working hard. Everything looked wonderful, bright and shining, with fresh coats of paint all around.

There were merry-go-round ponies for boys and girls to ride, and boats to steer around a pond.

There were cars that went z-zip! like the crack of a whip, around the loops in a track.

There were speedy little planes that whizzed through the air—and a roller coaster with the

highest climbs and the steepest drops and the scariest ride you could ever hope to see!

"Looks like plenty of fun all right," said the Flub-a-Dub, the talking animal.

"Yes, indeed!" said Dilly Dally.

And Clarabell Clown thought so, too.

So did the children! As soon as the gates were opened, they swarmed into the park.

Howdy Doody sold hot dogs and taffy apples as fast as he could count, and money piled up in his cash drawer—heaps and heaps of nickels and dimes.

Howdy was so busy that he did not notice Clarabell, who came creeping up, looking hungry as could be, to the hot-dog stand. All of a sudden he snatched the pile of hot dogs and dumped them into a big sack. Then away he ran!

"Stop!" cried Dilly Dally, racing after Clarabell.

But the bad clown did not stop.

Away he ran across the park, with Dilly Dally at his heels.

Soon they came to the pond where the little boats went round. Into the first little boat the bad clown jumped, and off he went.

Dilly Dally jumped into the next little boat, and away he started too. But the pond was crowded with little boats full of children going this way and that.

Dilly could not catch up with Clarabell. Soon Clarabell reached the far side of the pond and he jumped from his boat onto the shore.

He was running off through the crowds of people before Dilly Dally could dock his boat and start on the chase again.

"Stop thief!" cried Dilly Dally in such a loud voice that the Flub-a-Dub heard him far away. The Flub-a-Dub was over near the merry-go-round when he spotted Clarabell heading his way, with the sack of hot dogs tucked under his arm.

"Stop thief!" cried the Flub-a-Dub, but Clara-bell would not stop.

Instead he jumped onto a merry-go-round horse and rode away as fast as that sturdy horse would go!

The Flub-a-Dub jumped onto the horse behind. "Giddyap!" he shouted in the horse's painted ear, and the wooden horse quivered with eagerness. Up and down, round and round that painted pony raced, with the Flub-a-Dub clinging to his neck. But they could not catch the horse ahead.

Soon down jumped Clarabell, hot-dog sack and all, and he raced away again through the crowd.

This time he headed for the roller coaster, that airy scary speedy ride!

"Get out everybody!" he honked his horn. And everyone scrambled out of the car when Clarabell started to get in.

Then up, up, up the first steep hill he climbed, with the hot dogs beside him on the seat.

Howdy Doody saw him.

"Turn off the power, someone!" he cried. A brave little boy stepped out of the crowd and headed for the power switch.

Howdy Doody jumped into the nearest small airplane. Fast and faster, round and round he flew.

When he was going as fast and high as that small plane on its chain could fly, he pulled out of his pocket a Motordoodle and fitted it into place.

Then he reached up with his hunting knife and cut right through that chain!

Off into space Howdy Doody flew, with the Motor-doodle chug-a-rumming power for his plane.

Clarabell must be caught!

The brave little boy had reached the power switch by now. He took hold with both hands and pulled!

Clarabell in his roller coaster car had just reached the top of the tallest climb when, clink! off the power went. And there he hung in the middle of the air, with a dizzy sea of faces down below.

"I'll have to get out and push!" thought Clarabell.

So out he stepped—into nothing at all! And he hung onto the car with one hand.

Now when Howdy Doody came flying by, that bad clown was glad enough to be caught. He fell happily into Howdy's small plane. And he closed his eyes up tight.

Then down flew Howdy Doody to Dilly Dally, who took charge of naughty Clarabell.

Howdy Doody flew back for the missing hot dogs. And he tucked them in beside him in the plane.

"Okay!" he called as he circled round. "You can start the power now!"

Chuck-a-chuck! Tootle-oot! The power came on. The roller coaster rolled again. The planes whirled around. The ponies pranced. The small boats went swish! as merry as you please. And the hot dogs sizzled on the grill.

For the brave little boy who helped Howdy save the day, all the rides in the park were free all summer long!